WHO DID THAT?

Adventures with Odora the Skunk!

WRITTEN AND ILLUSTRATED BY ROSEMARY LINCOLN

Photo Credits: back cover, pages 1, 2-3, 32-33, 34: ©lumikk555 - stock.adobe.com

Produced by Beeline Media and Design, Inc. / Jason Register, President

Beeline MEDIA & Design

P.O.Box 1401
Titusville, FL 32781
www.beelinemediaanddesign.com

ISBN 978-1-7357254-0-6 (hard cover)
ISBN 978-1-7357254-1-3 (eBook)
ISBN 978-1-7357254-2-0 (EPUB)

Printed in the United States of America

— Based on a True story —

At the mall there was a pet store
With a sign upon the door.
"Baby Skunks for Sale" it read,
Just too much to ignore.

Once Mama agreed to buy one,
We children chose our pet.
So Odora came to live with us,
A decision we didn't regret.

We thought we would make her happy
With her own room in a hall.
Food and water dishes
Were placed along the wall.

To that we added a sandbox
And a gate that was very tall.
But Odora soon told us
She was NOT happy at all.
She pulled and tugged
The gate right off the wall.

6

She followed us everywhere
As we went about our chores.
But we had to remember
Odora could not go outdoors.

"Do you know you have a skunk at your feet?"
The frightened visitor asked.
"Well, yes, but you need not worry
And you need not run and hide.
Her smelly weapon has been removed.
You're welcome to come inside."

If you should come upon Odora
And wonder how to act
She will give you a fair warning
The first part of her attack.

She has very poor eyesight,
But if she feels afraid
She will stamp and stamp
Her feet at you
Before she tries to spray.

10

While facing you directly,
She'd turn her rear around
And aim her empty weapon.
But we could stand our ground.

Because the doctor didn't tell her
When she was very small
That he removed the smelly bag.
So, she has no weapon at all.

Odora went looking
For something fun to do.
She thought she'd play in the bathroom,
As that would be quite new.

"There is something very strange
About this white thing on the wall.
It doesn't go back up
when I pull it with my paw."

13

"There is a wonderful noise
When you open up this door.
Pots and pans come tumbling
As they fall upon the floor."

16

"Obviously these vegetables
need rearranging, too.
Mama will be so pleased.
She will have less work to do."

Odora is helping Mama
Get dinner in a pan.
She smelled her favorite vegetable
And figured out a plan.

Climbing up the ladder,
Odora reached the prize.
A big green zucchini
Was right before her eyes.

"Mama won't miss a zucchini.
She has such a big supply.
I'll help her with dinner
After I give this one a try."

Odora went trick-or-treating.

Not everyone was pleased.

Her friends got extra candy.

She couldn't spray but she could tease.

Odora found the open closet door.

"Now I wonder what's in here.
A broom, some coats, some boxes,
Nothing for me to fear."

"I think I'll dig a hole in this wall.
Who knows what I may find?
There might be some food, a place to
sleep, or a place where I can hide."

Mama was walking by the patio door
And was very surprised to see
A skunk she thought was Odora.
But how could that possibly be?

Maybe some careless child
Had opened up the door
And our sweet Odora
Had gone out to explore.

She started to open the sliding door
When suddenly she gasped,
"This isn't our Odora.
Her back is white as snow.
Odora has a black back.
This skunk will have to go!"

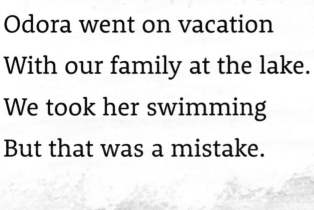

Odora went on vacation
With our family at the lake.
We took her swimming
But that was a mistake.

When Odora touched the water
She had never seen before,
She turned her body right around
And headed back to shore.

After swimming and after dinner,
Bedtime stories were read.
Then everyone would brush his teeth
And head right off to bed.

But Mama had a problem.
She put the book away.
She realized that Odora
Did not have a place to stay.

She looked around the cottage
And found a chest
with an empty bottom drawer.

She filled the drawer with towels
And many pillows, too.

But Odora wasn't interested
In being in the drawer.
She climbed right out, lickety-split,
And landed on the floor.

Picking herself right up again,

She climbed upon the bed.

She just wanted to snuggle and hug

With her family, instead.

You need not ever wonder,
What Mama thinks of you.
She will always love you,
No matter what you do!

About the Author

Rosemary Lincoln enjoyed a career of twenty-five years as a public school guidance counselor and English teacher. This is her first book. She lives in Vero Beach, Florida, and Nantucket, Massachusetts.

In Appreciation

I wish to thank Donald Russell, my fiancé, who kept me on the task of writing the book. He was my best critic and most loyal fan.

I wish to thank Ardith Schneider, who was most helpful with her encouragement to finish the book and with her great suggestions and references as to the rhymes.

Also, I wish to thank Ursula Gunter, who graciously shared her expertise in photography and artistic presentation.

Dedications

This book is dedicated to pets everywhere who enrich our lives and expand our thoughts beyond ourselves. They are loyal, affectionate, and entertaining. We marvel at their ability to solve problems, get what they want and need, yet they cooperate and conform to our rules.